This book is a work of fiction. Any similarity between the characters and situation within its pages, and places and persons, living or dead, is unintentional and coincidental.

Matilda Scotney has asserted her moral right to be identified as the author of this work.

Joy In Four Parts: A Sci Fi Novella

ISBN: 978-0-6487545-2-7

- *The First Part*

Today, I saw my face.

If today never happened, how would I know how green looked on grass or what blue meant to the sky? Without today, even though I believe in the sun, I would never gaze at a sunset, nor a sunrise. Daddy told me how the sun is a huge golden ball that hangs in the sky and warms the Earth. I have felt its warmth. He says the sky is so vast, it can hold billions of planets, but above the Earth, where we live, my family and me, the sky is a blue place full of fluffy clouds. Daddy couldn't describe 'blue', but to help me understand clouds, he placed soft wool in my clumsy hands, so I could 'feel' their fluffiness. When a child cannot see even shadows, there is only imagination to comprehend the wonderland that lives above her head. Daddy said the wind scuttled the clouds around, so he blew on my hands. I felt his breath flowing over my skin, and I imagined the quiet clouds hurrying out of the wind's way. Daddy painted beautiful mind pictures for me. He says Earth is 'phantasmagorical', which means even people like him, who can see and whose sense of touch is better than mine, don't always believe.

There were a few things I could touch. Daddy gave me big pencils to fit into my awkward hands so I could draw what I saw in my mind's eye. Daddy told me when I got it right or if I was close.

I have touched my parents' faces. My fingers tried to make out the contours of their chins, their noses, or their ears, but I never could, even when they described to me what I felt. Sometimes, Daddy rubs his rough beard against my face to make me laugh; I pretend to myself I can feel it, all wispy and tickly. I will miss Daddy's 'goat's kisses'; that's what he calls them.

When Sebastian, my little brother, was born, I worked out how faces grew and transformed, but Sebastian was born with eyes, and he can see all the things I cannot.

All my life, until today, my tongue was stilled, my eyes blind. My bones broke easily, so I couldn't run and play. I fell in the garden one time and had to drag myself back to the house because I couldn't stand. I felt no pain, but I knew my ankle, even with my limited sensation, had twisted. I don't know how it happened; my nerves never told me when something should hurt. Dr Daddy fixed my ankle, and I had to sit still for days. I didn't mind because Mummy read to me all the time and sang funny songs to make me happy.

Hearing and smell have been my only real senses. I saw so much through my parent's voices. Mummy's voice, sweet and light, and Daddy's, as if he puts a laugh in every syllable. When I put my ear to Daddy's chest, I can hear his voice rumble around.

Our home is in the middle of a farm so big; no-one ever comes to visit. In my mind, I picture our house as a pleasant house with lots of windows and a big kitchen where Mummy likes to bake. It is a house where everyone loves each other, where Mummy and Daddy keep Sebbie and me safe. Daddy sometimes gently rubs my fingertips against the wooden walls, but my stupid hands can't make sense of wood. I can't make sense of grass either, but I like it. I like how it smells. It smells of the entire world under my feet. The feet that before today, I could not feel.

I love to be outside when the sun is looking down, warming the world, giving the little plants life. I even got to know how far I could stray from the house. Daddy called it my 'perimeter alert sense' which I suppose makes up a bit for not having the senses of touch and sight. Daddy got me a dog to make sure that if my 'perimeter alert sense' broke, I would have someone to look after me to lead me home. Silky is a quiet dog. I love to brush her soft fur, but her softness never made sense to my jumbled-up brain.

Sebastian grew. I did not. Mummy said it was because I needed to have my food through a tube in my tummy. She said that is the reason I break so easily. Sebbie is four now, and I know he's not much smaller than me. Mummy said I was six when he was born, so I must be ten now, and I don't remember ever being any different.

Sebbie has learned to say proper words; his voice is tiny and sounds like it comes out of his nose. He tells me about the things he likes in the garden, his little voice punctuated by out-of-place breaths and questions of "see?" as he yanks my hand. But at that time, I couldn't see. Sebbie, with his baby understanding, would put whatever treasure he discovered into my hand, not knowing I couldn't feel it either. He asked me, only days ago, in his little boy's voice,

"Where are your eyes, Joy?"

We were together on our large settee, me in between Mummy and Daddy, Sebbie on Daddy's lap and Silky leaning against my legs. Daddy always smelt of clean shirts, Mummy smelled like floral perfume and Sebbie, well, he smelled like soap, except for his hands;

it depended on where he'd been putting them. Often he smelled like Silky's fur.

Daddy didn't want to discuss my eyes. I felt him sweep Sebbie into his arms, "Come on, young man, none of that," Daddy declared. Sebbie laughed at Daddy's bristly kiss as they left the room with Sebbie still giggling. Mummy hugged me.

"Are you okay, sweetheart?" she said very softly as if something had happened that made me need comforting. I didn't understand why. I knew I didn't have eyes. Sebbie was bound to mention it one day, the same as one day he would ask why I couldn't speak. But I heard the worry in Mummy's voice.

Yesterday, the sound of engines passing overhead woke me up very early, then there came hammering on the front door and the sound of a man shouting,

"Doctor Bell! It's Professor McNamara."

Then everything went silent. Mummy and Daddy couldn't be asleep, and I strained my ears to hear any more sounds. We had a rule; if someone knocked on the front door, we must not answer. We must stay quiet until the people went away. When the knocking started again, I dragged my blankets over my head.

"Doctor Bell. Please open up."

Didn't the man know that Mummy and Daddy were both Dr Bell? Mummy and Daddy hadn't told Sebastian about the opening the door rule; I guess they thought he was too small. I heard his little feet running down the stairs.

Daddy was furious. I had never heard his voice like that, and it frightened me. He was not angry at Sebbie; it was at someone else, and he used grown-up words I knew we must not say. An engine sounded in the front yard, waiting, like the getaway cars in the old movies Mummy and Daddy watch and describe to me.

A man shouted over Daddy's voice, but I didn't dare get out of bed. I listened to what they said. This was about me. About me not being able to see or touch.

Mummy came in and pulled back my blankets. "It's okay, Joy," she said. Her sweet, light voice sounded afraid. "There are some doctors here who have come about new eyes for you," she told me. "You'll be able to see everything we see. Won't that be splendid?"

Splendid? When it came with shouting and banging on the door and Mummy afraid? I am accustomed to not seeing, and these doctors sounded strange and important. And if they were there to help, why didn't my parents rush to answer the door? I didn't want to meet these people. They were the first visitors to the farm ever, and they didn't sound friendly, but Mummy wouldn't let me hide. She took me downstairs to where there were unfamiliar smells in the room, the odour of dark clothes, heavy perfume, and bad breath. The loud voices stopped when Mummy and I entered.

Bad Breath knelt in front of me. I visualised him with stubby limbs and wearing a large coat. He put his hands on my shoulder, gripping me hard, so I twisted away to reach for Mummy, but my hands couldn't find her.

"Um, Joy," Mr Bad Breath puffed out stinky words into my face. "I am Professor McNamara. We've been looking for you for a long time."

"Professor McNamara can help you see," Daddy said, but for the first time, I didn't hear a laugh in his voice.

I heard Professor McNamara's breath go in and out like he was thinking about what to say next. "Yes, I can," he said, agreeing with Daddy, but I could tell he didn't mean it, "and I can help you speak and stop your joints from cracking, but you will have to come with me." Then he stood and spoke to Daddy as if I wasn't there.

"It has never been exposed to other humans?"

"Never," Daddy replied, and he made a sputtering sound like he was really angry.

"That's marvellous, marvellous." Professor McNamara said "marvellous" twice. Isn't something marvellous only once? Can you make marvellous better? I didn't understand, and I didn't understand his next words either. "You took a chance having a baby while protecting an aberration," I heard him say to

Daddy. “What if …”

Daddy didn’t let the professor finish, “We don’t think of her as an aberration…nor as ‘it’.” He got furious again. His anger scared me, but Mummy knew, and this time, my hand found hers.

“So it seems,” the Professor said, “but we can’t have this aber...” he stopped to find words. “We can’t just let it roam free. You know that. If you wish, you may come with us. I am surprised such an oddity could bond with you both. If you prefer, you can leave it to us, and you can get on with your lives.”

“We’re coming,” Mummy’s voice had a sharp ring, and she pulled me close. “Joy is our child, regardless of any labels you put on her.”

“Dr Bell,” Professor Stinky Breath McNamara said, “Both you and your husband have breached several laws.” I put my hands over my ears. I wanted him to stop talking and go away. “These laws are in place to safeguard us all. ‘Joy’ is—I have to say it—an aberration, and we must deal with it. You are in danger of losing much more than just this defective if you do not voluntarily hand it over to us. As it is, you have kept it hidden for too long.”

I am defective. Inadequate. I learned then why we lived so privately in the middle of nowhere, why we have a rule about not opening the door to anyone. Not because

Mummy and Daddy liked solitude, but because they were sheltering me from a world that didn't tolerate differences. Now we'd been found out, and Mummy and Daddy, nor I, were to be given a choice.

"What will happen?" Daddy asked. He sounded so sad.

This time Miss Heavy Perfume answered, "We'll evaluate it. Then decide whether to allow it to continue."

"We'll get our coats and meet you outside," Mummy said in a shaky voice. She pushed me towards the stairs, and I heard the people leave. The engine outside was still running, waiting, hurrying us up. Those people weren't going to leave us alone. They were going to take me, a ten-year-old defective, still in her pyjamas.

"Nothing bad will happen, Joy," Daddy promised, and I believed him. "Now, you and Sebbie get dressed. We are going for a long drive, and you'll be able to hear for yourself all the things you hear on the broadcasts. Won't that be grand?" I didn't like his voice, wobbly like Mummy's and sad and pretending. But I nodded anyway. I was pretending myself.

Silky licked my hand. What about my dog? Would she be coming with us? We couldn't leave her behind. Who would feed her? But Mummy and Daddy didn't say anything about her.

I'm a big girl and capable of dressing myself, but Mummy wanted to do it. She made a fuss about doing my hair and talked about the city we would pass through. Now and then, she stopped to wipe her eyes. I didn't know what I had done to get Mummy and Daddy into trouble, to make them both cry and to have scary people at the house, or why I had been born without eyes if it wasn't allowed. Is not having eyes a crime? Sebbie howled, fearful of the sound of the engine that waited outside. When I touched the vehicle's door, it buzzed like a bee. I know what vibration is now. I didn't then. Silky barked at us as we got in; Sebbie curled himself into a tight ball on my lap, and we sat in between Mummy and Daddy as we left our happiness behind.

The journey took hours. Mummy still cried softly, and Daddy cleared his throat often. Professor Bad Breath said nothing to me, but when Sebbie got tired and restless, he described the passing scene to keep him amused. As Daddy promised, I heard the city, but not a small part like on the broadcasts; I heard it all; a chaotic cacophony that made me put my fists over my ears. I didn't understand loud, and it made my insides shake. It scared Sebbie too, and he wailed his fear right into my ear.

I heard birds singing. Birds only sing in trees, so

we must be flying as high as the trees, then other times, I thought we were travelling near the ground because I heard crickets making ticking sounds as we passed. I wish I paid more attention to those sounds now. It would be the last time I would ever hear them.

I wanted to tell Mummy and Daddy I wasn't afraid, even though I felt it, but I didn't have a voice. I know flawed is not good. Daddy is a doctor, and I wondered why he never fixed me. Then these people would have left us alone.

Daddy walked quickly; I think he knew where he was supposed to go. I smelled Professor Bad Breath and Ms Heavy Perfume walking with him. Mummy held my hand, and I felt the heat reflecting from walls and structures around me. Sebbie was silent, and I didn't hear his little feet running to keep up, so someone must have carried him. Not Mummy or Daddy because Sebbie's soapy smell was beside me, higher up. Someone else was holding him.

"Joy?" Daddy stopped and put his hands on my arms; he spoke into my face, so I knew he was kneeling. "This is the last part of the trip," he said. "We have to go on a special aeroplane." His voice was calm and slow, like when he wants Sebbie to understand. "I've told Professor McNamara all about you, and he thinks he may be able to help."

The laugh in Daddy's voice hadn't come back,

but I knew he wanted me to nod to show I understood. I didn't then. I do now. The other people were quiet, expectant. For what? For me to react. If I could speak, I would have asked about Silky.

I didn't like flying. There were too many belts that crisscrossed over my chest, over my arms, over my legs. I felt trapped, even though we weren't as squished like we were in the first vehicle. I wondered if we would be flying near the sun. I could smell Mummy and Daddy and Sebbie close by. I heard other sounds too, and voices and clicks, like the sound lights would make if they blinked. Do blinking lights make a sound? I didn't know. Not then. I do now.

After the special aeroplane, we went to a room that echoed with clangs and clatter. Daddy stood to my left and Mummy to my right. Professor McNamara came close to give me another blast of his bad breath. He didn't like saying my name.

"Er, Joy, this is Dr Shea."

A voice said "hello", a woman's voice, a young voice that made me feel its owner didn't think of me as defective. "Dr Shea is a specialist," Professor McNamara said, "she may be able to make you more acceptable to society. We can't promise, though..." then I heard him say under his breath, *"This is unbelievable"*. He turned his voice away as he spoke to my parents, "You know you can't continue the way you have, don't you?" He was asking them, but I thought the question was for me as well.

Then, I didn't know what I know now. All I knew was that I lived with Mummy and Daddy. I had a little brother and a dog called Silky. Why couldn't I stay as I was? I had never hurt anyone. I was happy. I couldn't see or feel things properly, but Mummy and Daddy loved me just the way I was. But when you are only ten years old and have no voice, it's hard to ask a question or to challenge. I thought about struggling and running away, but Mummy and Daddy were already in trouble because of me. When Dr Shea took me by the hand and led me away, I knew my family and everyone else was watching, and even though I couldn't see them, I turned to look.

I know eyes have colour, Daddy told me, but even with all his mind picture painting, he could not prepare me for the wonder of Dr Shea's eyes. When I woke up, she was leaning over me, her mouth tilted up at each corner. Is this a smile? In amazement, I felt my mouth copy hers. And her eyes, what was this phantasmagorical colour? Just before I went to sleep, Dr Shea said she would give me speech too. I knew words, and now I can try to use them. Ask about the colour, ask about Silky, my brain urged, but the words felt alien, buzzing around on my tongue and flying about my lips like flies. I opened my mouth, and all the words gushed out in a heap. Dr Shea's mouth curved again, and she stepped back for me to see the other people in the room.

I know that is Daddy; I recognise his beard. Mummy is standing next to him. Their mouths are smiling. Sebbie is watching, but he isn't smiling. He is frightened. Mummy pushes past a man standing close. That is Professor Bad Breath, who has a bad breath face as well. He steps aside.

"It's alright, sweetheart," Mummy's sweet, light voice is all the more beautiful because now I can see how her mouth shapes those words. It makes her happy to see me smile. "You'll get used to speaking, Joy. Dr Shea is going to be with you every day to help you."

Dr Shea? Not Mummy? She spent lots of time when Sebbie was learning to speak. Why do I need Dr Shea? Are they leaving me here? Is Daddy happy? He looks happy. Does this mean I am no longer defective and can go home?

Do you remember the moment you first felt your eyelids blink? I wanted to touch my eyes, feel the lids flick up and down, but I couldn't lift my arms. Dr Shea loosened the restraints. What are these things all around me? Are these machines? Is that a wall? If I touch it, will it feel like wood? A moment ago, I could only imagine lights. Now, I can see the brightness Daddy tried so hard to explain. When I got to see the sun, it will be like a light in the sky. I wanted to ask them to show me blue, so I can know blue when I go outside and see the sky, but I couldn't say it. Words are funny. They tickle.

Everyone in the room had colour in their eyes. I wanted to see my eyes, but clumsy mouths form clumsy words, only Dr Shea understood. She asked if I wanted to play a game. I'm ten. I like games.

"I'll get a mirror, you close your eyes," Dr Shea made a big smile, "and when you open them, you'll have a surprise."

My mouth made smiles at Mummy and Daddy while we waited for the mirror, but I turned off the smile when I look at Professor Stinky Breath. Soon, I would see myself for the first time, no longer defective. Dr Shea cured me. She said so, and when the mirror arrived, I gripped it without it falling from my hand.

I knew then why I had never met other children and why my parents kept me a secret. It is because I am not like them.

Today, I saw my face for the first time.

I am not human.

- *The Second Part*

Peter Mallory almost dared not to enter the lab. His heart was in his mouth, well, not literally *in* his mouth, he always thought that was a ridiculous saying, but it was beating hard in his chest and felt like it was heading towards his gullet. He swallowed a few times to make sure it stayed put. Mallory fantasised about this moment for most of his life. This part of the base was off-limits, but security on the moon installation was pretty slack because there was no way off unless you had a ship, and he looked official enough that no-one stopped him or challenged his presence. If anyone asked, he would say he got lost. He looked the part; medium height, balding, a single ocular prosthesis and an official badge that declared a level one security clearance, the lowest level.

Mallory knew where he'd find it. His old man told him the location of the lab where it worked but that it was locked in, that he'd only be able to see it through the window. All his life, Mallory heard of the two Dr

Bells' cybernetic achievements from his dad and how one of their later experimental androids spontaneously developed a personality. Now, barring someone questioning his presence in this part of the base, he would get to see it. With a bit of luck, he may even get to look into the legendary eyes. Mallory wiped his face, glancing down at the smear of moisture on his palm. Why would this make him sweat? Because he was tiptoeing around where he had no business being? Or because the enigma of the android had intrigued him since childhood, even inspiring him to a career in science and engineering himself, although his dad took all the credit for his son's decisions. Or maybe it was because few risked censure to see it. Despite his career aspirations, Mallory had only ever become a second-rate shipyard design engineer, not even far enough up the food chain to warrant a place on this mission had it not been for the death of another crew member, leaving an urgent need to fill the position.

Mallory's father described the corridors accurately. It appeared not much had changed in twenty-five years. Mallory decided a long stride with feigned confidence would be less likely to draw attention, not wishing to tip off any surveillance cameras or staff he might bump into, although the few he encountered scarcely gave him a second glance. He shifted his eyes right and left, working under the notion that turning his head might give him away as someone who doesn't know where he is going.

Mallory found the door. It was easy to see through, and he expected it to need a code, something he didn't have, to get through, but to his surprise, the door slid to the side. Expanding his award-winning performance as a man not out of place, he stepped through with a daring he wondered if he would regret.

The door slid closed behind him, and he swung to look, making sure no-one had followed him. At that moment, his courage failed. His bravado ration used up for the day, Mallory felt too timid to turn back to the room in case he came face to face with the object of his inspiration. He stared at the door, castigating himself for his craziness and for building up the android to such an iconic level. The Terran Android Regulation Office, or TARO as it was commonly known, jealously guarded the android's achievements, and over the years, released little about it to the public. Mallory believed the android to be behind many technological advancements, but TARO took all credit for its triumphs, playing down its remarkable accomplishments as a collaboration with human scientists. Everyone knew that was crap and just posturing by TARO. One hundred and fifty years ago, the android developed an engine coil that decreased the time it took to travel between Proxima Centauri and

Earth, and sixty years after that, TARO announced light speed as a barrier to deep space travel, was formally broken. While they had several ships capable of reaching the speed of light, they only had one ship in operation capable of SOL4. That was the one they were using for the terraforming mission, on loan (at enormous expense) to the Arisi Confederacy, a philanthropic organisation. Mallory guessed the android wasn't idle in those intervening years and speculated about its other inventions and developments not yet shared with humanity. It was because of the android, the mission he had just joined could travel to the most distant planet any expedition had visited before, and though things might go pear-shaped, he didn't have much reason to come back; his sister maybe, but she would understand.

Mallory took a deep, calming breath and turned slowly. The laboratory was darkened and hushed, save for the sound of water trickling into a sink. Creeping a few steps forward, Mallory found himself in the centre of the lab.

"Are you lost?" A few lights came up as a female voice spoke from somewhere above his head. Mallory looked up to see a blue face peering down over a railing on top of a narrow spiral staircase. Mallory shuffled further into the lab, keeping his face upturned to the android. In turn, it kept its eyes on him.

“Er, no,” he stumbled over his words. “I was looking for you.”

“Then it appears you have completed your objective.” The android stared for a moment, then turned aside before moving from his sight.

“I’m Peter Mallory,” Mallory called out. He couldn’t see where it had gone. “I’m part of the terraforming team to Calladere.”

“Congratulations,” came the caustic retort from somewhere at the top of the stairs.

“I developed the gas…the um, housings, well not actually the housing, but the portable…” Mallory stopped babbling. He always turned into a moron when he was nervous.

The blue face once more appeared over the railing, “Are you here for anything specific, Mr Mallory?”

“Um, yes,” Mallory lied. He hadn’t got beyond the notion of seeing the android. Any form of conversation had not been part of his lateral thinking. “I require…I need your advice with the canister placements in the cargo bay. They’re fragile, and the contents—as you designed the ship we’re using, I, we assumed you would know the most strategic positioning to launch them from orbit, you know, prior to landing. I don’t fully agree with the current specs.”

Mallory heard the android’s footsteps as it

descended the stairs. It was probably coming to view the complete idiot gushing out nonsense and kick him out on his ear. The android came to stand before him. Mallory knew they'd added length when they remodified it a couple of centuries ago, but it stood at least a head above him; a little shorter would have been less intimidating, for Mallory at least. The android looked him up and down. He could sense it appraising him, weighing up what it saw, perhaps reading his heart rate, his blood pressure, checking out what he had for breakfast, tracking every gurgle on its progress through his bowel, and if he needed to take a dump or a pee. It could probably even see the size of his dick. God, Mallory thought, why would he think it would even be interested in his schlong? It was an android, for heaven's sake, but its blue humanness made him jumpy. And it's blonde hair. No other Bell android had hair, nor did they have startling, wide blue eyes.

The android blinked once and trailed a circle of tiny particles in the air, waiting a moment as the particles solidified. It handed the resulting disc to the visitor.

"These are the specifications. I extrapolated the dimensions from the plans of your portable housings. They'll be straightforward to install once you are underway."

Discussion over, the android moved away, but

Mallory had waited his whole life for this moment. He couldn't let it go just yet. Summoning uncharacteristic bold initiative, he followed, "Um, I've read about you," he said, hoping to sound intelligent and wise, but his voice didn't come out as he planned, his vocal cords only delivering a squeaky, "You look incredible, I mean, in real life." Mallory bit his lip. What was he doing, chucking it a pick-up line? What next? Let's have a drink and get to know each other better?

The android stopped at the bottom of the steps. It didn't speak, only kept its back to him as Mallory continued to babble about the android's accomplishments, which of course, it already knew. Babbling on was a weakness of Mallory's, not an endearing trait either and one likely to cause the environmentalists on the terraforming mission to turn him into a shrub. Still, he couldn't let this moment pass, even if he had lied about why he was here.

"My dad worked here; he…"

"I remember him."

"You do?" For a moment, Mallory was shocked to silence. Unfortunately, it didn't last. "Oh, I suppose you've met thousands…"

The android spoke over her shoulder, "I'm guessing your father told you about me, and it inspired you to come looking?"

"Um, well. Not just to come looking, since I was

a kid, you know, stories. They brought you up as a human. Is that true?"

He didn't see the android blink a couple of times. That same question, whenever someone made it to the lab, over and over. The android began to walk up the steps, Mallory trailing after it. He'd asked a direct question, and the rules were that if you ask a Bell android a direct question, it had to respond. The Bell's wrote those rules, and this was one of their inventions, so it had to count.

"Mind your own business," the android retorted as it ascended the steps to return to its work.

Mallory stopped halfway up the stairs. He supposed that technically it had responded. It hadn't answered, but it did make a response. In ineffectual helplessness, Mallory stared after the android that had undoubtedly learned to fudge the rules over the years. Flapping his hands a couple of times, Mallory backed away and started down the steps. This meeting had not gone as he'd hoped.

"For nine years."

Mallory dared not take another step. He made a furtive glance to the side and saw the android studying him with its extraordinary eyes. Encouraged, Mallory turned and looked up.

"You believed you were human?" he asked.

The android's full mouth sloped somewhat in

mild amusement. "When you were a child, Mr Mallory, did you think to question whether or not you were human? Was any evidence presented to you either way?"

The smile more than the question disarmed him, and he took a moment to answer. "I guess I saw I was like other humans."

"I couldn't see, nor did I have a fully developed sense of touch," the android told him, "nor could I speak to challenge my existence or origin. How could I have known? My parents and I lived in isolation. It was here I discovered I was not human." The android looked around, "Here, in this laboratory. Until then, I didn't know my lack of those senses made me less than human."

"My father studied cybernetics," Mallory said, "only as a hobby. He said you had a dog."

Mallory had no idea why he asked that. It was irrelevant. He should ask it about its work and achievements, but no, the fool asks the most intelligent android in the galaxy if it had a dog.

"Silky," it answered after a moment, then returned to its work. Mallory took a few more steps up the winding staircase so he could get a better look. The android was female-looking, more so than he'd expected, long legs clad in elegant slacks, padded velveteen slippers covering its feet and a long white tunic that reached to its thighs. Looking at its blue-tinged skin, the darker v-shaped shading between its chin and forehead, he found it easy to remember it was not human, but he'd discounted it also had feelings, a phenomenon that made it so unique. And he'd reminded it of something it had lost.

"I'm sorry," he floundered, "Did I upset you?"

"No."

"It was just that for a moment…you had a melancholy look on your face, you know, a sad memory, sorry."

"I am an android. I don't have looks on my face."

"No, of course. Well," Mallory decided it reasonable now to withdraw. It wasn't going so well, anyway. He'd seen it, and that was a feat in itself, plus he was still standing halfway up the stairs, staring at her, and decidedly not in the position of authority he thought he'd have over an android. And it hadn't invited him in. "I'd best go," he stated without moving. "They've assigned me a pod; I understand they're pretty strict about mealtimes and things. Isn't the accommodation compound where they've installed the artificial atmosphere you designed?"

It glanced at him, the soft overhead lighting diffusing the pigments in its blue skin, generating little sparkles all over its face. Mallory got the feeling his stalling had turned into a source of amusement.

“That’s true,” it said. “If you don’t turn up at mealtimes, you become the meal. I recommend you hurry.” The android made a ‘hurry along’ movement with its hands.

“Yes,” he grinned stupidly. Did it just make a joke? He nodded. “On my way. Just leaving.”

But he couldn’t bring himself to leave. How could he walk away from this technological marvel, this remarkable triumph of engineering? Mallory racked his brain for a few other suitable adjectives, then settled for “unlike any other android ever devised and never again to be duplicated”. His first description—technological marvel, turned from its task and, in an irritable gesture, crossed its arms.

“Still here?”

“Uh, do you live at the pods?”

“I live here,” the android replied tartly. “I do not need separate living accommodation.”

“But you’ve been on Moon Base for two hundred and thirty-three years. You just live here?”

“Correct.”

“You’ve never set foot outside this place since they brought you back?”

“Correct.”

“Even when you were designing the ships? The artificial atmosphere?”

“I design, others build,” it said. “I respect the

technicians and engineers on this base. They have my full confidence."

Mallory nodded and searched for something else to say, something that wouldn't put his foot in his mouth, but he didn't have such sophisticated conversational skills. "Don't you get lonely?" he blurted out. A few moments ago, he asked it about its dog and was positive he elicited an emotional response, albeit by accident; he was never unkind, not even to androids, but now, he'd asked another personal question.

"I thought you were leaving," it said as it took a step towards him.

And this time, he left.

"I can't believe it, Jenny!" Mallory squawked at the holographic image of his sister, his arms flailing as if seeking to ward off a swarm of bees. "It's incredible! All my life, I wanted to meet it, and now…"

Mallory's younger sister made a few grand and futile attempts to respond, but her brother wasn't listening. He had just realised a lifelong dream, and he was "staggered"—an expression he used repeatedly in his portrayal of the android. "Staggered" by the detail of its body, "staggered" by its voice, although he conceded the personality side was a bit lacking—he guessed he'd built himself up for that letdown—but it was so articulate! Mallory spewed out the minutiae to his sister, almost running out of breath on a few occasions, "…and guess what?" he added, his eyes wide. "It's blonde! It has blonde hair and these incredible blue eyes! And a helluva figure," he made an exaggerated feminine shape in the air, which made his sister groan.

"Are you planning on screwing it?" she laughed.

Mallory stopped his delirious ravings, "What? No, of course not. It's just that it looks like a blue woman. Well, not blue, blue. It's pale blue, but from the chin to the hairline, there's a deeper blue v-shape; I don't know if that's an aesthetic added by its designers or…well, no-one knows. They were going to destroy it, you know?" Jenny knew. It was all her brother spoke about for the last year, since he knew he was going to the moon base. "What a loss that would have been," he gushed. "Artificial atmospheres, greater than light speed coils. It's brought humankind a long way in only a bit over two hundred years."

Mallory hesitated, taking stock of what he just said. "It's odd; humankind didn't invent the things that—you know, furthered humanity, but a machine did it, a machine that once believed itself to be human. Jenny, did you know it had a dog? We never had a dog."

"I knew the Bell Mark Four had a dog, Pete,"

Jenny said. "Dad told us, but it had that dog over two hundred years ago, and we didn't have a dog because we classify them as a protected species. Anyway, enough about the android, how are things revving for the terraforming mission?"

Mallory forced himself to answer his sister's uneducated and irrelevant questions. He knew she was indulging him; she had no interest in science, and she knew he knew that, so, in the end, Jenny blew him a kiss.

"I'm going. Love you."

Mallory sighed as the transmission ended. He and Jenny were friends rather than sharing a proper brother/sister bond. He'd deliberately missed out telling her he might not come back from Calladere, but she had her own life, and even though she'd miss him, she'd get over him soon enough.

Mallory wandered out to the artificial atmosphere garden to check it out. Anyone who visited Moon Base was welcome to partake of all it offered, which amounted to nothing except terrible food, cramped quarters and a pervading sense of desperation from everyone to get to someplace else. This visit was Mallory's first to the moon; he'd spent his career in a shipbuilding space dock in Earth's orbit. For most, the idea of going to the moon was enthralling, but the early excitement of those individuals was quickly cured.

Unless they were TARO employees, people rarely sought a second visit unless transiting to Proxima Centauri or Mars, where the living conditions were little better than the moon. The artificial atmosphere installation made big news on Earth and in the outposts, and he expected it to be in full use by station personnel. It surprised him to find it deserted, considering such a development had implications for future colonization. Mallory guessed it didn't hold sufficient interest for jaded travellers to expend much time. The single Speed of Light coils never engaged between Earth and the moon, so the trip always took a couple of hours, so if you were heading home from Proxima Centauri or Mars, which still took months or weeks depending on your ship, a crew was always eager to get off the moon's transit hub.

The garden was no bigger than a good-sized lawn, a few hardy flowers trimmed the edges of the green-in-a-brown-sort-of-way grass, and two trees had enough foliage to look like their planting had been a success. The whole experiment had been encouraging enough for TARO to programme a Bell Mk II android in horticulture. Right now, it was busy pottering about the garden and looked up at Mallory as he stepped into the zone, its face blank and its eyes, well, it didn't really have eyes. So different from the startling features of the Mk IV. A slight haze emitted from the generator some ten meters above, but he'd read the Mk IV was working on clearing that issue, and when it did, the stars overhead would shine through. He looked forward to visiting it during the day when the moon had some sun on its surface. Even so, the artificial sports-arena-at-night look didn't detract from his respect for what the android created. To be able to go outside on the moon without protective gear was a remarkable achievement. He hoped the terraforming mission would green up the proposed area of Calladere, but unless they were diligent, with only shallow roots and fragile plants, it could be a catastrophe waiting to happen. His responsibility was to filter out the toxins on-site, but if they could sterilize the entire area prior, it would make it that much more straightforward. He glanced up at the atmospheric generator. Something like this would shorten the mission and allow faster growth. This terraforming expedition would be the first undertaken by private enterprise. The others, all endorsed by the android's owners, TARO, failed, but then, they'd never let the android accompany any terraforming teams. Mallory secretly thought this mission might just go the same way. Terraforming was a monstrous joke amongst the general populace, enough to make him wary of sharing details of his new job with anyone.

Mallory's head remained tilted back, staring up at the generator. The device wasn't big, and part of it biological, but how the hell did it *work?* TARO would never part with the science, but he wondered if the android would. He could ask it, although that might be over-inflating the impression he made. Waltzing in with a "hey, remember me, your friendly neighbourhood drop-in. Fancy sharing the specs on the atmospheric generator?" probably wouldn't work. The android might even stomp on his head. Then Mallory had an idea; perhaps he could coax the Moon Base Director to loan the android to them. They'd hired other equipment from TARO, it would cost, but he'd gladly donate his salary, and for a moment, he felt a rush of excitement that quickly punctured. What they paid him for this mission wouldn't be enough to rent the android for an hour. He could appeal to the Director to petition TARO on behalf of the mission as it was for a philanthropic organisation. They might consider leasing the android, provided they guaranteed to return it with Captain Ty. The Captain wasn't staying on Calladere anyway. TARO didn't want it's only SOL4 ship away for that long, but Mallory wasn't in charge; he was only there by default. Ty would have to be the one to approach the Director.

Hurrying back to his pod, Mallory grabbed his personal comm gear and headed towards the Director's office. It was worth a shot. He wasn't as overawed by the Director as he was the android, so turning up at the

Director's office didn't cause him the same apprehension, which was fine, but he hadn't considered the time difference between the moon and Earth. Ty's sleepy, unshaven, angry face swam into view. His hair was a mess, and he looked like he'd been in bed for days. The prone figure of a naked woman lay on top of tangled sheets on a bed in the background.

"Mallory, what the fuck?"

"Oh, Ty, sorry," Mallory focused on Ty's face. "It's important. Look, I met the Bell Mark Four. I've seen the artificial atmosphere it designed. It's created a park here on the moon; grass, flowers, it's got a garden seat..."

"So. Fucking. What?"

"We're terraformers, Ty. We'll have an area of five square miles to terraform on Calladere, and it will be under an artificial firmament, it won't let in sunlight, it won't let in the rain, we may just as well terraform on Neptune. But if we had an atmosphere..."

"Oh, god, Mallory," Ty groaned. "You want the android?"

"We need the android, Ty. It would guarantee success."

"They'll never let it go."

"Only on loan. Offer them something in return. They never let it out of its lab."

"It's got a personality or something, doesn't it?"

Ty said, rubbing his eyes. He'd only met Mallory once, and already he hated him. "Maybe they think it's capable of turning rogue. There's been a couple of Bell androids gone crazy over the years."

"This one hasn't in two hundred and thirty-three."

"Okay, what does the Director say?"

"I'm outside his door now. I thought you would be better to pitch this to him."

"Mallory, you…" Ty shouted as he saw Mallory press for admittance. He lowered his voice. "Mallory, I'm the pilot," he hissed. "I only got to command this expedition because none of the rest of you can fly. Once you are all established, I get to come back, and you guys take your chances for five years."

"I know, but you also don't sound like a moron when you're asking for something. I do."

From what Ty knew of Mallory, his self-appraisal was spot on. Still, Ty doubted his ability to make a compelling argument about borrowing TARO's most prized possession. While he hesitated, Mallory spoke into the Director's office control and was admitted.

Ty patted down his hair and sniffed his armpits even though it was only a face-time call. He scowled at Mallory as he tightened the field of vision so the Director couldn't see the naked female still languishing on his bed.

Sprawled in his office chair, Director Vox

presented a picture of a soft, pudgy splodge of boredness. This diversion was welcome enough, he thought; the moon was the perfect spot to numb one's mind, so a visit from one of the terraforming team taking the Bell Android's SOL4 coil ship for a long spin at least brightened his day, or was it night? He checked his watch. He'd forgotten to wear it. No matter, after the first week, it all became one long day anyway.

"So, Dr Mallory? From the terraforming team? What can I do for you?"

Mallory opened his comm gear to reveal Ty, who'd taken those couple of seconds to put on a vest. Director Vox took the comm from Mallory and squinted at the dishevelled man on the screen.

"Director Vox," Ty recovered himself well, proving Mallory's confidence in him as a worthy petitioner. "I'm Captain Ty, piloting the terraforming mission to Calladere and commanding until the team set up the base. Mallory has a proposal."

Mallory made wide eyes at Ty, warning him only he, as mission commander, had the authority to make such a request. Ty was sure the Director would shoot the plan down in flames. Still, he took a deep breath. He wasn't a scientist, but the addition of the android, even if its presence on Calladere was temporary until he returned, might just work to his advantage.

"The Bell Mark-Four," Ty continued. "Mallory reckons it'd make a great addition to the expedition. Our sponsors, the Arisi Confederacy, would compensate you, and of course, the android would return when I return."

Vox looked from the screen to Mallory, then back to Ty and burst out laughing. He hadn't used that laugh in a while. There wasn't much to amuse on the moon. The laughter felt good. It made his feet tingle.

"Is this a joke, Captain Ty? You must know she's not mine to barter with?"

"She?" Ty shot a baffled glance at Mallory.

"I believe it identifies as female," Mallory told him; he didn't feel like owning up to the Director that he'd met the android.

Ty's expression changed to one of disbelief. "Well, that's not common knowledge. TARO certainly likes mysteries."

"The android doesn't leave the lab, Captain," Vox said. "Unlike the earlier Bell androids, which require maintenance, she carries out self-diagnostics and upkeeps herself. Basically, we leave her to her work, which ensures TARO continues as world leaders in technology. Do you think TARO would let such a valuable piece of equipment out of its sight?"

No, Ty agreed silently, they'd be crazy to, and Ty had said so to Mallory, now he looked like a clown for asking. He vowed to keep Mallory in his place in the future.

"Any hiatus," Vox continued, "however useful in the cause of terraforming, would be a loss to the scientific community the android serves closer to home. I'm sorry, but I can deny this request knowing I have the full backing of TARO."

Mallory had assumed the android was under the base's direct command, but he should have known that more widely, it would involve TARO. The Arisi Confederacy had secured two other Bell Mk-IIIs for the mission, which were no substitute for the Mk-IV. Mallory had no way of knowing if the Arisi Confederacy had ever considered asking for the Mk-IV, but he knew the difficulty the Confederacy had in securing the SOL4 ship, even on a lease.

Ty scratched his ear. He was only dropping these crazy adventurers off, and he shouldn't be getting involved in this. "Thanks, Director. It would seem Mallory here is a little overzealous."

Vox smiled, "It's no problem, Captain. Sorry I couldn't have been more helpful."

The screen snapped off, and Vox leaned back, tilting his chair and lifting his feet onto his desk. The chair groaned and cracked dangerously, giving Mallory visions of picking the Director off the floor, perhaps with the stalk that supported the chair stuck up his backside.

Vox raised his eyebrows and looked Mallory squarely in the eye.

"Really? That was your idea?"

"The android is wasted here."

Vox ignored him. "I say again. Really? You expected me to ask TARO if you can borrow an irreplaceable asset? Does this look like a library, where you can check things in and out? What if they damaged the android? Or destroyed it? We'd all be implicated in the fallout, including you, my friend."

Mallory backed towards the door, "I guess I didn't think it through. The two Dr Bells made their androids to benefit society; I just thought having the Mark Four at the forefront of terraforming would serve society too." Mallory hesitated, "Don't you think you should let it out occasionally?"

"To do what?" Vox gave a contemptuous laugh, "Sniff the air? Smell the roses? Mallory, we're on the moon. The only atmosphere we have here is the few square metres the android herself invented. So far, she hasn't been able to extend that."

"Well, I'm sorry to have taken up your time." Mallory bowed briefly and left. Vox waved a hand in dismissal and returned to the business of tedium. At least the last few minutes gave him a laugh.

Outside the door, Mallory sighed. It would have

been amazing to have the android along, but at least he got to meet it. And why the hell did he bow to Vox?

It was another of Mallory's unfortunate traits that once he got an idea in his head, it grew, or festered, or did something; either way, this idea would not let him rest even after he convinced himself he'd made peace with Vox's decision. A plan to ask the android what it thought about going on the mission began to germinate. Night mode had descended, so with few people about, he wandered back towards the lab. There was no sign of the android, and the room was in semi-darkness.

"Hello?" he called into the gloom. "Er…hello? It's me, Peter Mallory."

"I'm in here." The android's voice drifted from an anteroom at the top of the staircase. Taking the response as an invitation, Mallory climbed up the steps and, seeing the room, peered in. The android was seated in an armchair, naked from the waist up, a conduit running from a cylinder into a port in the android's side. Mallory's jaw fell at the sight of the android's utterly perfect blue breasts sitting atop a tiny waist. Recovering himself, he stepped back in embarrassment, turning aside and mumbling his apologies for the intrusion. It brought back the awful memory of the time when, as an awkward teenager, he walked in on his parents having sex. Now, as he did then, he fumbled about for somewhere to hide his blushes. The android laughed.

"It's okay. I'm a robot, not an actual person. You can come in."

Mallory took a moment to garner his courage before lifting his gaze.

"I'm sorry, I didn't..." he continued to fumble with words.

"These accoutrements make me look more human," the android said, pointing to its breasts, "so I could blend in when they finally let me out in society—" It stood and withdrew the tube from its side with a popping sound, "—then they shut me up in here for two centuries." It grinned at him, "Go figure."

Mallory pointed to the cylinder, "What's that for?"

"It keeps my surface covering supple. Without it, this—" the android took Mallory's hand and brushed it against its soft, pale blue midsection "—becomes brittle and affects my neurological responses and dexterity. So, every couple of months, I get to sit around and drink." It pointed to the armchair, "Sit."

Mallory obeyed, and the android elegantly crossed its legs and sank to the floor opposite.

"Do you ever get downtime, leisure?" Mallory asked, feeling that the moment of intimacy allowed him some liberty with questions.

The android laughed again, a normal-sounding, soft laugh that made him smile. "Why would I need downtime? To expand my mind? Perhaps I could go to the base library and pick up a romance novel!" It made a show of frowning in thought, "Hmm, something erotic, maybe, titillating?" It raised its eyebrows, "Now wouldn't that be fun!? Or perhaps a horror story." It looked about mysteriously and lowered its voice, "I could turn out the light in the lab and scare the life out of myself. Oh, wait," it held up a finger and grinned, "maybe not, I'm an android, I don't feel emotion, nor do I have any life to scare."

Mallory deserved that. He was a master at awkward conversation, but he really only wanted to know one thing, even though he didn't know what kind of reception the question would get. Right now, the android appeared amiable.

"Do you ever think about leaving?" he asked.

Again, the bemused expression preceded the answer. "Is that an offer to smuggle me out in your backpack? I can fold myself up, but I expect a leg here and an arm there might still be visible."

Mallory cringed, "No, I asked, or rather my captain asked Director Vox if we could borrow you for the terraforming mission."

The android's extraordinarily blue eyes widened, "Did you now?" It looked at Mallory from under long, dark lashes. It had a remarkably expressive face, despite it saying it didn't. He even thought it was impressed. "What did he say?"

Mallory pretended not to feel overcome by the fact that he was now engaged in a conversation with the Mk-IV. His mother once told her shy, bumbling son that to be bold, you might have to pretend. So he tried to show some confidence, some chutzpah. "What do you think he said?"

"That TARO would not agree," the android snorted, "that I'm too valuable, yadda yadda yah?"

"You're right, but I thought I'd ask how you felt. You're the only sentient android in existence."

"And they're too afraid of me to let me out." The android held his gaze. Its eyes went beyond simply complementing the blueness of its skin; their cerulean depths held more, so much more than the nothingness of the other more basic Bell androids; these eyes had personality, humour, warmth. Mallory sensed it was appraising whether he feared it too. *I'm not afraid,* he said to himself, but he knew the android could quickly become an obsession. Had he considered it, he would have realised that the tipping point had already come and gone.

"They think you might be unpredictable," he said.

"Because I smashed a few windows when I was new? Broke a few technician's legs?" The android nodded, "That was before my father connected me to the cerebellum. I did not understand what I was doing."

"Wasn't that the reason they terminated the programme? Because you were capable of anger?"

"Humans are capable of anger," the android pointed out, "and they walk around like they own the place."

"But you can't be controlled the same as humans. Even so, it doesn't seem fair to keep you in here for a misdemeanour."

It studied his face. He knew nothing, but his adoration amused the android. "It's not the only time I've rebelled," it admitted. "There were a few more incidents over the years." The android casually lifted a perfectly contoured shoulder, "Part of my programming is the protection of humans, and another part is free will. The two don't always pair up that well."

"You don't seem violent, you seem…" Mallory didn't want to say the word. It wasn't a word he ascribed to himself, but…

"Normal?" the android grinned. "Except I'm two-tone blue to make sure I'm easily distinguishable. My parent's other creations didn't have hair and only given rudimentary eyes. Heaven forbid we would upstage humans."

"Would you consider coming with us?" Mallory didn't know where that came from; he was almost tempted to look around to see if someone else had joined them because the voice was too bold, too forthright. But it was his, possibly about to make the mistake of a lifetime. The android blinked twice and waited while he found more to say. "Could you petition TARO?" he added. "We could use you."

The android tilted its head, "What if I say no? I might love it here."

"Because until I met you and walked around that little garden you designed, breathed in the atmosphere, I believed we had everything we needed for the terraforming mission." Mallory shook his head. "Now I see we don't. We're missing a crucial part."

"Little old me?"

"Yes, little old you."

To Mallory's surprise, the android took a deep breath. He recalled nothing in the articles he'd devoured over the years about it breathing, probably an affectation to make it seem more human. Somehow, that made its incarceration even more cruel.

"They won't let me go, Mr Mallory," it said after a moment. "I have considered just walking out, but—" the android pointed to its face, "it's not as if I can mingle. I tried once to change the colour of my skin to make it more human-looking. It proved harder than formulating the SOL coils."

"What if you didn't change your appearance?"

Mallory's brain continued to fire on impulse. "Say you just escaped, and I hid you on our ship?" Mallory didn't yet know where he was going with this, nor had he considered the impact of his words.

The android blinked, reaching up to fidget with its blonde curls, stretching down a ringlet and letting it bounce back up as it considered Mallory's proposition.

"No-one's ever asked me to run away with them before," it said. "And no-one guards me, although TARO has placed a useless perimeter alert which I modified years ago. That's why you made it into the lab. I could do it, you know, leave if I chose."

"I'd have to smuggle you onto the ship immediately before we depart," Mallory said, his idea gaining momentum and he overestimating how much he would actually have to do to break out the android. "When it arrives, it'll be docked at the landing bays at the far end of the base."

"You don't need to do anything," the android said, and with that, Mallory became forever entangled in the theft of TARO's most valuable asset. "I'll do the smuggling," it said. "Just expect a knock on the door."

Mallory's heart slammed against his ribs, and sweat popped out in beads on his forehead. The android had agreed to something he suggested. He could never return home after such a stunt if they pulled it off, but he never planned to anyway. By the time TARO was in a position to pursue them, the android and Ty would have returned. And Ty? Well, Ty would have to take whatever came his way. Mallory knew TARO would put two and two together when Vox told them about their conversation. The expedition had the fastest ship, and the other SOL4 coil vessels were years from completion and testing.

The two misfits sat in conspiratorial silence for several minutes, each considering their role in this crime.

"Did your designers always plan for you to be female?" Mallory said when the silence became too awkward for him.

"I'm created in the image of my mother as far as the blonde hair goes," the android said. "I'm taller now. They changed out my lower limbs and made me a little more proportional."

"I read about the limbs, but not the…" Mallory made an uncomfortable patting gesture against his chest, a move that caused the android to grin. "Um, breasts," he stammered. "You consider the late Dr Bell, the cyberneticist, your mother?"

The android inclined its head. "Both Dr Bell's were my parents. I called them Mum and Dad."

"Uh, yes, of course. What did they call you? I can't imagine they went around calling you 'Mark Four' all the time."

“Yes,” the android said, smiling. “They did give me a name. They called me Joy.”

- The Third Part

I have a close relationship with the SOL4 ship. I invented it, I designed it, so I guess you could say I'm its mother, but unlike some kids when they move out of home, it kept in touch, even though TARO believed that once they built the prototype, they severed any link the ship had to me. Yeah, right? As if I'd let that happen. I know what disconnection from your creator feels like.

Humans. They think they know everything. That SOL4 ship is my baby. When the nurse cuts the umbilical cord, human babies keep their bond with their mother. It's no different with the SOL4. I created it, like I created all the other systems on this base. Believe me; they know their Mumma. A word here, a cascade shift there, and the SOL4 coil is in on my new adventure. It knows it's not going to Calladere and that where we're going will take a bit longer, so it's fixed a course change out past Neptune. The pilot, Ty, won't get to come back to Earth as planned. No matter, he'll cope. I'm not bothered about being tracked; the celebrated scientists on this base have no idea the entire power hub is another of my buddies and has agreed to go down a few minutes after the SOL4 leaves. No comms, no light, no launch facilities, ergo, no way to follow, the base will be helpless in the dark. I'd love to be a fly on the wall as TARO debate their prudence in leasing the SOL4 to the Arisi Confederacy.

That odd fellow, Peter Mallory, came by yet again last night, this time to make sure I was still planning on joining the mission. I've convinced him we'll make it look like I'm a stowaway. He doesn't know my real plans, but he'll find out at the same time as the rest of the crew. Mallory's one of those who finds it difficult to fit in; he won't socialize before launch, so no opportunity to blab.

I've adapted the payload field parameters to extend to the outer hull. I can survive in space for quite a while, but light speed will strip my skin, so if for some reason I don't get into the ship, the field will buy me some time. I won't attach to the hull until just before the ship is due to leave. Once I'm inside, I'll commandeer the mission. I would have preferred not to have the humans along, but there's not much I can do about that.

When I told Mallory I never contemplated escape, I lied. I contemplate it every day. I also lied about never having left the lab. I do it all the time. As I said, the power hub and I are besties, and it's nice to have a wander; I make sure no-one sees, and it eases the tedium. Just for fun, the power hub and I once collaborated on a full schematic to blow the moon base to smithereens. I wouldn't do it, but the fact I have that capability is amusing. If a cyberneticist came to study me, it would take years to discover the algorithms of my overactive imagination.

There, I'm all set. The SOL4 ship is in position, and the crew is aboard. I can just imagine Mallory's crewmates wondering why he's twitching with nerves — they'll discover soon enough. Base power is down in 10 minutes for night mode. I've got enough serum to keep my skin supple for several thousand years. I'll take Mum and Dad's picture, the one with Sebbie and me, Sebbie's arm over Silky and her tongue lolling out. It's my favourite, the one they left me when TARO sent them, my family, back to Earth. Mum and Dad called me on face time as soon as they got back.

I hated to see my mother cry, and I hated TARO for not caring how much they hurt her and Dad and Sebbie. Silky was still at the farm when they returned, even though they'd been away three years. She survived by catching rabbits and drinking from the dam. I have thousands of screenshots, so I can relive our facetime. Over the years, on our facetime calls, I watched my parents grow old, I saw other dogs join the family and pass away or go missing, and I watched Sebbie grow up. Then there were two face times, Mum and Dad, and Sebbie at the Academy; he didn't facetime as much when he graduated. Years went by, and there was just Mum, then one day, when we were supposed to talk, she wasn't there, so I sent an urgent message to Sebbie. He took leave and went back to the farm, where he found her, sleeping. She'd been sleeping for days and would never wake again. Sebbie made sure she and Dad continued their long rest side by side in the ground, under the grass.

Sebbie married and had kids, they liked their Aunty Android, and later, Sebbie's kids had kids, and theirs had kids, and now I guess I'm just a family story or maybe completely forgotten. When I invented holocalls, there was no-one left who remembered me.

But I don't forget. TARO took my family, and now it's my time. With a few tricks I've kept stored up my sleeve for just this occasion, I've set the new SOL coil engine manufacture back decades.

Illumination's down, and the base is in night mode. Ghosting features are in place to make it look like I am in occupancy, although I know no-one will come looking for me. Had TARO built the SOL4 on the moon, I would have done this years ago. Imagine snatching *that* from under their self-righteous noses?

Anyway, I love sneaking about and performing tiny acts of sabotage on the base; with TARO so sure I influence none of their systems; no-one suspects me.

Not a soul in sight. Recognition light ignoring me as programmed, each door panel sliding noiselessly to let me pass, just as I told them. There's something to be said for power, and there's no power like seeing a ship you designed just waiting for you to climb aboard. It's there, out on the launch pad; sleek, unique, like me. And like me, it is blue. Blue mother, blue baby. The engines are initial sequence backlighting, so the launch pad is clear. The ship is waiting for me. It's folded up a side strut for me to grab and slide my way around onto the underside of the ship; I can settle into the deep contour built-in for attaching the runabout when working in space. I told Mallory to make sure it got stashed in the hold.

I feel like laughing at the ease of all this. Mallory the Simple was so keen I come along, then, when I agreed, he turned jittery and droned on and on about how hard it would be for me to get away. Well, not so far, and with this level of magnetisation to the hull, it would take a nuclear explosion to dislodge me. Secondary ignition is underway. Good. I scheduled the power to drop out on the base as we clear atmo. A few thousand clicks further, and comms will drop; when that happens, I'll knock on the access portal and invite myself in. You know, don't you, I don't have to knock? The ship will just let me in, but doesn't everyone dream of a dramatic entrance?

"What the fuck is that tapping?" Ty slapped the flight desk and yanked out his earpoint.

Fuller, the co-pilot, screwed up his face and listened hard, "Nothing here," he said, but he could hear nothing above the comm traffic and secondary ignition. The two always rattled his sensitive eardrums. He was a blow-in like Mallory and not an experienced co-pilot, so he was trying to focus only on what the Captain said.

"There's tapping coming through this earpoint," Ty yelled, banging the tiny device on the console before examining it. "Can't anyone else hear it? Shit!" he threw his hands up in irritation as the comm traffic went silent. "Now comms are down. God, this is gonna be a nightmare. Retrace, Fuller, we're going back. This ship might have bigger issues than things that go bump in the night and faulty comms."

Mallory jumped up, "No! Um, don't do that, Fuller."

Ty turned in his seat, his face dark with anger. So far, they were less than an hour into the mission, and everything was already going wrong. He didn't need that little upstart Mallory belaying orders.

"No, sorry, Captain Ty." Mallory raised his hands

in defence, "It'll be fine. If we go back, they'll quarantine us because we got through the atmosphere. We don't want them delaying the mission. I'll go track down the tapping."

Ty frowned. Not like Mallory to be helpful, and he wasn't the type to interfere with a direct order even though he did show some guts in going to the Director about the Bell android. Still, every time Ty looked at Mallory, he had the same two thoughts; the first that Mallory was an idiot and the second, why did the Arisi hierarchy send an idiot on this mission? If Mallory continued to irritate, he might find himself in an airlock accessway and blown into space. Didn't sound so bad; Ty could make it look like an accident. He filed away the image for future study and returned to the matter at hand. The other crew had flight deck tasks until they engaged SOL4, so Mallory was superfluous when it came to crew.

Ty nodded, "Okay, check it out."

"What about comms?" Fuller said, awaiting directions. Fuller considered Ty a somewhat mercurial sort and lousy leadership material, but the Arisi Confederacy, despite claiming to be a philanthropic organisation, quietly liked shady elements they could manipulate with money. Ty was one of those, but undeniably, he was a great pilot. Fuller knew it would take more than downed comms for him to abandon a mission that paid well, but Ty was not known for tolerance; a persistent tapping noise might just push him over the edge. Even so, Fuller knew Ty would retract his order to retrace.

“Do you want me to try contact with Earth?” Fuller suggested. “Their systems might be operational.”

“No,” Ty huffed out his breath, “It’s probably just a glitch.”

“So, carry on?”

Ty reconnected his earpoint, “Yeah, carry on.” Ty wished they’d found a proper co-pilot to replace the one that missed his flight; Fuller seemed to be as much use as Mallory.

Mallory trod the periphery gangway where artificial gravity was minimal and only used to access the upper airlock. The ship had amazing power resources that would keep it flying for hundreds of years. Even so, TARO insisted power had to be conserved, just as it insisted on a flight deck, despite the ship being capable of flying itself. But humans were suspicious of mech that operated outside their control, so a flight deck was duly added.

Ty’s response to the tapping would be the least of Mallory’s problems, and as he once again pondered his recklessness, one look at the upside-down grinning blue face that dangled from the upper airlock hatch made him momentarily glad his common sense had taken a back seat. She would ensure their success.

"Hello, Mallory." The android flipped herself over and stood in front of him.

"Hello, Joy, I can't believe we're doing this. Ty lost it just because of the tapping."

"Did he?" Joy's face lit with delight. "I thought that was a nice touch. You know I could have overridden controls?"

He didn't know that, but the knowledge, and the fact she mentioned it, caused Mallory a brief moment of consternation. What started as an idea to install an artificial atmosphere might be him unleashing, at worst, a sociopathic android on the universe, at best a mischievous trickster. The android dusted her hands. "In a few seconds," she said, "the ship will turn command over to me, and Ty will have no choice but to comply."

"Turn the ship over to you?" Mallory fell in beside the android as she strode towards the flight deck, hardly able to believe what he'd just heard. "Wait, Joy, are you going to hijack the ship?"

"Where the fuck are you, Mallory?" Ty's voice echoed on the internal comms and bounced off the bulkhead. Another voice murmured something calming in reply; that was Fuller. Joy knew him, he worked as a resident physician on Moon Base, but a few hours of space travel got him this gig in place of the selected crewman who mysteriously didn't show. Joy smiled to herself. Ty already believed this mission was jinxed. Well, she'd make it better. Flashing a smug glance at Mallory that stopped him in his tracks, she stepped onto the flight deck.

"Oh, dear," Mallory groaned. "What have I done?"

Joy knew which members of the crew had received flight training and would be on the flight deck. Aileen Williams, General Science Officer, sat at the science station—the ship told Joy it would need to compensate for her inputting errors. Boris Jupp, Head of Botany, Carly Bolt, Climatology and Environment (identified as the crew member most likely to resent Joy's presence) and Liz Evans, Bacteriologist. Twenty other specialists, ranging from cloning experts to horticulturalists, were in stasis, along with a number of animal embryos and insect larvae. Fuller and Mallory completed the flight deck complement. Mallory only remained on deck because they didn't want to waste the single remaining stasis pod they might need in an emergency.

"We agreed I would pretend I'm a stowaway," Joy whispered, giving Mallory one last glance before all hell broke loose, her vivid blue eyes shining with mischief. "You know nothing."

Mallory knew no way would Ty believe that, not after the conversation with the Director, but he also wouldn't believe Mallory would have the balls to break the android out. Heart in mouth, he followed Joy onto the flight deck, knowing full well joy was not what she'd be bringing.

"What the fuck!?" Ty leapt from his seat, and Fuller swivelled around to stare in surprise at the blue android. No-one mentioned it would be joining them.

Ty clenched his fists and yelled, "Mallory!"

Mallory peered from behind the android, shrinking as Ty made an aggressive move towards him. Joy stepped between them. "Mallory only told me about the mission, Captain Ty. Stowing away was my idea, and since you like the word 'fuck' so much, Captain, fuck off." Joy pushed past him towards the controls, and Ty made the mistake of grabbing the android's shoulder to stop her,

"You can't do this!" he shrieked. "I'm in command. Mallory, where's it's off button?"

Mallory maintained his distance, flapping his hands and looking stunned, gestures which, fortunately for him, persuaded the crew of both his idiocy and his innocence. Joy turned her head ever so slightly and beneath lowered lids, glanced at the hand on her shoulder. She didn't like to be touched. A violent surge into Ty's body sent him zapping across the deck onto

Bolt's lap. Ty pushed himself to his feet, dazed but still willing to fight. Joy saw it.

"We can do this the easy way or the hard way Captain Ty," she said evenly. "Your choice."

Ty rubbed his hands together; the tingling hurt. He knew little about the android, but he didn't doubt it could cause significant damage. He needed to think, play along, so he gave it a slight nod of affirmation.

"Good," the android said, giving everyone on deck a bright smile. "We are on a terraforming mission, correct?"

"Yes, but Ty's supposed to be in command," Jupp said, looking to the others for support but making sure he stayed safely behind his console. "You know, don't you, TARO is developing SOL4 coil vessels even now. They'll catch you, eventually."

Joy permitted herself an evil smile. This was fun! "No, they won't," she told him, "I bugged the schematics program. It'll be years before they work it out."

Fuller put up his hand. Mild by nature, he was happy to follow whoever was leading; it just took him a moment longer than the others to realise what was happening. "Is this a hijacking?" Right now, he felt more curiosity than fear, but he wanted to be sure he got things right. He'd seen the android on rare occasions but never heard it speak. Even from the little

Fuller knew, it would probably make a far better commander than Ty.

Joy sat down in the pilot's seat, "In a way," she waggled her blonde head from side to side, "more like taking back something someone else thought was theirs."

Fuller raised his hand again, "Did anyone brief you on the mission parameters? You've been in that lab for over two centuries."

Joy dropped her hands into her lap, "Don't worry, Fuller," she smiled, "I can call you that, can't I?"

Fuller nodded, dumbfounded by the android's startling eyes. He hadn't paid attention before.

"Good," Joy said. "So, tell me everything you think I don't know."

It was too much. Ty could not, would not stand by and let a machine rob him of his command. He slapped the back of the android's chair hard and spun it around, risking another zap.

"Who the hell do you think you are?" he snarled, shooting a glance at his co-pilot, "Fuller shut up. Listen," Ty spat, his finger raised to the imposing blue-faced robot who occupied the chair he believed was rightfully his. "You can't just waltz in and take over. The Arisi Confederacy invested billions in this venture; they won't take kindly to you stealing their investment and their property. TARO leased this ship to them. We are your masters. It's not the other way around."

Mallory had retreated to the doorway. He swallowed hard while he waited for Ty to go flying through the air again, but he was more concerned for himself. His life would be intolerable if the crew discovered his involvement in the android's plan. Hijacking had never been part of the discussion, even though he convinced himself it had been his idea for her to come along. Only later would Mallory realise the android had used him.

"Commander Ty," Joy said, fixing a steel-freezing gaze on the captain. "I designed this ship. In fact, every ship presently in operation between Proxima Centauri and Earth have components designed by me, from their coil systems to the quality of their toilet paper. The Arisi Confederacy doesn't scare me, nor do I have any allegiance to TARO. None of us is coming back. If by some amazing stroke of luck, someone develops a SOL4 engine of their own, one that equals mine, your bones will already be dust, so it won't matter."

Ty shifted his furious gaze to Mallory, who backed himself into the corridor, but on this ship, there was nowhere to run. To Mallory, the android seemed creepily reasonable and less cordial than before, well, not less, she had never really been warm, but she also had never seemed aggressive. Maybe aggressive wasn't right either; assertive would be a better fit. Or…Mallory stopped his brain rummaging through appropriate adjectives. The truth was Mallory felt responsible for the hijacking. He should have left well enough alone, but he just had to see the android for himself.

As Mallory suspected, Ty singled him out to blame for their current plight.

"Did you tell it you asked the Director to borrow it? I don't buy that stowaway bullshit," he hissed through teeth clenched in anger while he shoved Mallory into the corridor, baling him up against the bulkhead out of sight of the android.

"I—I may have," Mallory stammered, glancing toward the flight room in the hope Joy would come and rescue him. Ty was about to beat him to a pulp. He was convinced of it.

"You *may* have?" Ty twisted Mallory's shirt front, "You idiot! Mallory, we're not soldiers, we're not cyberneticists, so we can't take that thing down. It's got the strength of twenty men. You've put us all at its mercy, and it's taking us to fuck knows where."

"She knows what she's doing, Ty. She's…

"It, Mallory. It's an 'it'.

"You need to give her…it, a chance. Like you say, you can't take it down."

"And you believe it? You believe that ultimately, it'll have our best interests at heart?"

Mallory nodded, although the android wasn't acting as he expected. "I didn't bring her on board, Ty. She did that herself. I didn't help her get out of the lab."

Ty thrust his sneering face into Mallory's, but he let him go, then stomped back onto the flight deck. The crew were still at their stations; from what he could tell, not one of them had challenged the android. It occurred to Ty he was the only one who saw what was really happening here if the crew allowed it to continue. A mutiny. A mutiny that followed a hijacking. He eyeballed the crew, then pointed at the android.

"Are you all just going to accept this? An artificial lifeform as Captain?"

Joy had listened to the exchange between Ty and Mallory in the corridor. If Mallory came under any real threat, she would have stepped in. No way would she tolerate violence on her ship, and the moment would soon arrive when Ty would learn just how low he rated in the popularity stakes.

Ty walked over to the Head of Botany, "Jupp?" he said.

Jupp raised his hands; he would not take on the android. Besides, he didn't care who led them; he had a thing with Williams, so he would be happy anywhere in the universe. Ty turned to Williams, who shrugged. She hated Ty, but she always got on with Bell androids, although she'd never encountered one this sophisticated. Ty looked at Bolt, who just held his gaze. He didn't know it, but Bolt had a thing for "bad boys" in general and Ty in particular. Ty then went across to Liz Evans, who said simply, "Sorry, Ty, don't look like we've got a choice."

Ty didn't bother asking Fuller. He was another Mallory as far as he was concerned. Okay, so the crew prefer to follow the android. Ty knew it would never allow him the runabout to return to the moon, so he flung up his hands and walked from the flight deck. Joy smiled. How unexpectedly entertaining and satisfying.

We are not going to Calladere. We are going where neither TARO nor the Arisi Confederacy will ever find us. I don't believe even Ty thinks I'm stupid enough to allow TARO to track the ship. During the eighty-five thousand and one hundred-odd days since they took me from my mum and dad, did they think I was inventing stuff and enhancing systems to benefit humanity? Hell no. No-one checks my lab, so I calibrated everything on the base from the toilets to the deep space telescopes for me to sabotage or use, except with the bathrooms. It would be petty to disrupt such an essential human amenity, but I often patch through the lunar telescopes to my lab.

My sight can calculate far beyond anything human eyes can, but I haven't shared my findings, nor all of my abilities. Calladere might be ripe for terraforming, but there is another world, a better world, where they won't find us. The world has a catalogue reference, X01334. X because it's unreachable without SOL4 engines and 0 because there are others closer amenable to terraforming, even with the limited terraforming knowledge science has so far developed. It means X01334 is so far down the list of worthy worlds as to be buried. I haven't told the crew, who still barely speak to me since I returned the ship to its own control. Only Fuller and Mallory have anything to say. Ty won't be happy, but that doesn't matter; he's going into stasis if he keeps acting up. He won't like that either. I can hear him swearing from here, even though I confined him to quarters. Fuller is the only one who noticed flight coordinates are different, but he wisely kept quiet. He knows the ship and I are buddies, and he's accepted it. I like him. I like Mallory too, although I feel a little guilty about him. He's starting to wonder about me.

"Mallory, over here." Mallory was alone in the hydroponics bay. The bay was usually Jupp's territory, but Mallory got assigned minor maintenance when the senior officer was off duty. He looked around before he found the source of the fierce whispering. It was Ty, hiding behind the cabbages. Ty had behaved himself since the ship engaged SOL4. Joy always carried out any threats she made, and Ty had been at the pointy end of too many, so he mostly did as she told him. Mostly.

"What are you doing?" Mallory joined Ty behind the vegetables.

"The android," Ty gave the rest of the bay a furtive glance, "it's confined me to quarters again, but you need to stop it."

"Me?" Mallory's eyes widened. "Why?"

"Because it isn't taking us to Calladere, and it trusts you."

"Where is she taking us?"

"X01334, in uncharted space, you idiot!" Ty

gestured as if this were something the android would have confided to Mallory. “I had to pull some sneaky moves to get that info. Mallory, if it takes us there, we’ll never be found.”

“I don’t much care where she takes us. I wasn’t coming back from the mission, anyway.”

“Well, that’s fine and dandy for you,” Ty spat, “but what about the rest of us? We don’t want to live out our lives as colonists.”

“But, Ty, we are pioneers. That’s what terraforming is about.”

“Listen, Mallory. I’m going to be honest with you because I think you’re the only one who can change this situation around.” Ty went to place a hand on Mallory’s shoulder. It was too familiar, too false.

“Okaay,” Mallory drawled uncertainly, rotating his shoulder beyond Ty’s reach. Where was this going?

“I was supposed to return from Calladere after a few months,” Ty said. “Right?”

Mallory nodded.

“Well, I was going to leave a month early. There’s a Confederacy ship rendezvousing with me at Makemake. Their engineers were going to try and extrapolate the SOL4 engine design, I would return to Moon Base on time, and the Confederacy engineers would develop a SOL engine of their own. TARO lets no-one close to the ship, but Arisi engineers have devised a way to get a look at the engine."

"I suppose they'll pay you well for this bit of industrial espionage?" Mallory said.

"Of course," Ty frowned at him as if he were stupid, "But I'll get more if I hand over that blue-faced android."

"And I suppose you think she'll just let that happen?" Mallory almost laughed. Ty was no match for Joy, physically nor intellectually. "Besides, why are you telling me this? It doesn't look as if you're going to make that rendezvous."

"I'm going to turn this mission around if it's the last thing I do," Ty replied, thumping his fist against a hydrating partition, causing a splutter of water to spray the two men." But I can't do it alone. Bolt is the only one on side at the moment. Jupp and Williams will join us if we have a specific plan, and Evans will follow everyone else. If you help me make that meeting, we'll share fifty-fifty on the Confederacy payout."

"And you reckon Joy doesn't know you're not in your quarters?"

Ty made a glassy, I-know-better-than-it face, "It thinks it's clever. I know a few things about ghosting a system, and it trusts you, so you need to distract it so we can organise a flight deck lockout and return the ship to manual. I know how to do it."

"How do you plan on containing her?"

"Get it outside and attach it to the hull."

"How?"

"I don't fucking know, Mallory," Ty shook his face into Mallory's. "That's your department."

Mallory stood, blinking. Ty or Joy, Joy or Ty? Calladere or God knows where? God knows where or Calladere? Did Ty really think this would be a contest?

"No."

Ty was aghast. "No!?"

"Well, I have nothing on Earth to go back to," Mallory said plainly, "and all you do is drink and fornicate. You'll be able to do that anywhere we go."

Ty gritted his teeth. Ordinarily, he would have punched the stupid prick's teeth out by now, but he needed him. Ty didn't feel like negotiating, but the need to tread carefully was obvious right now. "Look, Mallory, it—she has gone rogue. She disabled the SOL program on Moon Base, and fuck knows what else to escape. Who's to say she won't kill us all if we piss her off. She might enslave us, make us work for her."

"You mean like we do to androids on Earth?"

Ty was losing patience, "You stupid..." He closed his eyes for a moment and took a calming breath. "Androids aren't realised. This one only pretends she is. It's learned behaviour."

"She had a dog," Mallory told him, "and a mum and dad. And a brother. She loved them, and TARO sent them away."

Flecks of foam appeared at the edges of Ty's mouth, "It didn't fucking love them, you fucking idiot! It's just a mass of circuits!" He narrowed his eyes, "Mallory, think. If that's true, then what if she's out for revenge and we're the schmucks she's going to take it out on?"

"She's nice," Mallory said, defending his friend. "She won't harm us."

Ty stepped back, suddenly suspicious, "Are you banging it?"

"What?" Mallory exploded. "No! I'm not sure she's even capable."

"You mean you've thought about it?"

Mallory shook his head. "Of course, I haven't. What I mean is, harming us doesn't appear to be her motivation. I think she wanted to escape the moon and free herself. Whatever way you look at it, Joy is sentient, and she was in that lab for over 200 years. You can't even stay in your quarters for a week."

"Well then, I guess we can count you out of our little band of rebels and count you in as the enemy?"

Mallory shrugged, "Do that, but you won't win."

"Says you, Mallory the Tosser."

"No," Mallory looked over Ty's shoulder. "Says Joy, the one in charge."

The android stood behind Ty as he attempted to

embroil Mallory in his scheme. She knew Mallory wouldn't betray her, the little trained monkey that he was. Joy knew he wasn't as smart as the mech on the moon, which obeyed her every command but also, he wasn't stupid enough to not be on the side of the winning team.

Mallory watched as Joy reached out and picked Ty up from behind, catching one leg and one arm behind him. He followed as Joy carried Ty to the medical bay where a startled Fuller was setting up his practice.

"Put him in stasis," Joy said, dumping Ty onto the examination table, waiting while Fuller administered the prestasis prep. As Ty slipped into unconsciousness, Joy left, ordering Mallory to remain to make sure the stasis happened.

"What's going on?" Fuller asked, checking out Ty for any injuries that might need treating before stasis.

"Ty was plotting a mutiny," Mallory told him. "Joy's not taking us to Calladere, and he had some sort of deal to allow the Arisi Confederacy to copy the SOL4 engine. I reckon Joy's off to suss out the rest of the crew."

"I knew we changed course," Fuller admitted.

"Why didn't you tell anyone?"

"I thought it might create panic. The crew have to

accept her, but they're uneasy. Wherever we end up, she's hardly likely to create a democracy."

"You don't know her, Fuller," Mallory defended Joy for the second time that day. "She's not like that."

"I know," Fuller grinned. "I don't mind her. God, the crew are screwed if they're thinking of joining Ty."

"I'm glad you think like that, Fuller. TARO made a monumental mistake in letting Ty lead this mission. Any of us would have been better, but Joy is better than all of us."

Fuller smiled, "You admire the android?"

"More than that," Mallory admitted, "I like her. I think this toughness is just mopping up the dissent she knew would happen when she hijacked the ship. You weren't thinking of dissent, were you?"

Fuller laughed. "Me? Heck, no. I'm like a river, I always take the path of least resistance, and I'm with you, she's okay to me, and I don't like Ty; he's rude and arrogant. The women don't like him either, apart from Bolt." He looked down at the sleeping Ty. "This is a vulgar man."

"He accused me of having sex with Joy," Mallory said.

"It's the only way to have it."

"I mean with Joy, the android."

"I know what you meant," Fuller laughed, "just lightening the mood. Here, bring over that stasis tube;

we'll strip him and get him in."

The two washed the unconscious Ty and applied his skin prep, taking a moment to have a few unkind sniggers about his anatomy, which they decided would lack appeal once a female conquest got past his facial features and roguish ways. Only in the bedroom would they discover his genital amplitude or lack thereof.

As the resident troublemaker transformed into an icy popsicle and with all systems reading normal, Fuller and Mallory went to the crew common room to listen to Joy's address.

"I have changed our heading. We're not going to Calladere." Joy's announcement caused a breakout of bewilderment and panicked questioning. She held up her hands. "We're going to X01334, in a system that has a sun and several planets, at least two of which are habitable, with some help. We have terraforming equipment if we need it. I believe you can make a comfortable life there."

"That planet is only newly catalogued," Williams said. "We know nothing about it, plus it's much further than Calladere."

"It is much further," Joy acknowledged. "This journey will take eleven months."

"But that's another seven months on top," Bolt stepped forward, stopping short of getting in the android's face. "We don't have sufficient rations. We'll end up using all the plants meant for terraforming."

"No, you won't," Joy assured her. "I brought nutbeads. Several thousand of them. If you substitute nutbeads for two meals, the rations will last beyond the time we need."

Evans looked at the others, her cheeks burning as she fought tears. "How long will we be there? I have parents and brothers and sisters. Don't you think you should have asked us before you made a course change?"

"All astronauts assume a risk when they go out into space," Joy reminded her. "And as to how long you will be there? Permanently."

"Permanently?" Evans's hand went to her mouth, and tears spilt onto her cheeks. "Our assignment to Calladere was only for five years," she sobbed, "just long enough to establish the development. Then there would be a change of personnel. They'll never find us where you're taking us. We'll be lost!"

"The assignment has changed," Joy said firmly. "We aren't just going to terraform; we're going to colonise."

Bolt put her arms around the weeping Evans, "You've taken everything from us," she snapped at Joy, "Everything. Our freedom, our lives. You are a machine; how can you understand how this is for us. You…you have no feelings, no conscience."

"Yes," Williams chimed in, "We're helpless. We can't refuse; we have no way to escape. We're trapped. You haven't just hijacked the ship; you've hijacked...*us!*"

Mallory felt the charge in the atmosphere, the disbelief and shock. He looked at Joy, who stood still, her magnificent eyes gazing steadily, just as she did when he asked her about the dog. She understood how it felt to be separated from family, the heartbreak of being removed without choice from everything she knew, but here, she was doing it to others, and that was something Mallory did not understand.

The implications of establishing a colony dawned on the crew. They would carry out their terraforming to supplement a planet Joy assured them was habitable with a bit of help but also knew a natural consequence of colonisation was children. With only a total complement of twenty-six crew, it didn't add up to much of a gene pool. As the days wore on, the women feared becoming baby-making machines, even though Joy tried to explain that would only be a part of the requirement and that she had considered the gene pool issue. She assured them their expertise placed them in the unique position of forming an intelligent society, one that would reach maturity at a rate far greater than Earth. She tried to convince them they had the potential of founding a remarkable civilisation. They wouldn't listen, choosing to believe Bolt's explanation that the android had malfunctioned and was just as likely to send them into a sun or a black hole. Bolt assured them Ty would sort it out when he woke up.

All the talk of reproducing presented a dilemma for Fuller. He was gay. The only gay man on board and a possibility Joy had not considered.

"Fuller's not going to be much help if you plan on increasing population, Joy," Mallory said when he had the chance to speak to her alone. "At least not naturally." He shook his head, "The women are right. You are violating our rights. You've kidnapped us, and eventually, if we want our species to survive, the women will be obliged to procreate with males they wouldn't ordinarily have chosen as mates."

Unencumbered by sexual desire, Mallory's point forced Joy to admit there were certain things she didn't entirely understand and some contingencies for which she hadn't prepared. "None of you will be required to have physical relationships if you don't choose," she said, "but man has a powerful survival instinct. There is no going back, and I do not believe they will want to die without leaving a legacy."

"I hope you're right," Mallory said, "I had little to contribute on Earth, and I admit to a certain anticipation of establishing a new world, but…Joy, did you think this through?"

"I accept I have much to learn," Joy treated him to one of her intense gazes. "What about you? Do you feel like an abductee?"

"Volunteer, abductee, either way, we're headed into the unknown. I had no plans to return to Earth." Mallory tilted his head, "I ask again, Joy. Did you think this through? Did you believe what you were doing was okay? Moral?"

"You don't know me, Mallory."

He shook his head, "I do know you, Joy, and I'm fairly sure your parents would have ensured malice didn't feature anywhere in your programming. I think you're seeking to replace what you lost. I just hope it's all worth it." And before the android formulated a clever answer, Mallory walked away.

Mallory is wrong. I am not seeking to replace what TARO took from me. I am motivated by revenge, and these humans are collateral damage. The SOL4 ship had never visited the moon before. Had it done so, I would have taken it then. I don't need humans. I have been without human company for over two centuries. Why would I crave it now?

No. This is vengeance. Without me, TARO will no longer be world leaders in technology. In removing myself, I have levelled the playing field. No longer will

TARO crow about *my* achievements, taking them as their own and playing them down as scientific progress *in collaboration* with the Bell Mk IV. When we left Moon Base, every trace of my research, designs, specifications, every classified and non-classified crumb of information was wiped from the computer files, courtesy of my chum the data matrix. Also, I deleted X01334 from the catalogues.

But I will make my humans happy. They didn't ask for this, and in saving myself, I took on a responsibility, just as my parents did when they wiped my memory and made me their child. I will make it up to the humans. They will thrive and grow. I will make it worth it.

- The Fourth Part

The designated landing area of X01334 was in the throes of a freezing winter. The gale-force winds kept the crew on the ship for a month before it warmed up enough to set up a camp. By the time they awakened the other specialists from stasis, the crew had resigned themselves to their fate. Their acceptance paved the way for the others, understandably bewildered at first, accepted Joy's leadership with little opposition. The specialists took up the tools of their trades, quickly bringing the local landscape under control. Only Carly Bolt bucked, which resulted in Joy removing her from the community and confining her in quarters on the ship. Boredom brought Carly around eventually, but she was simply biding her time until they revived Ty, who was still in stasis. Joy felt he had little to offer the colony, anyway, save muscle. Bolt, however, was confident Ty would deal with the android and rescue them. The fact he'd failed spectacularly before so far hadn't registered.

As the winter landscape cleared, they discovered areas with natural springs, a freshwater bonus that was quite a cause for celebration. Joy found a protected lakeside area that trapped warm air from the sun during the day and afforded a balminess to the evenings. The pleasant location encouraged the settlers to relocate. The SOL4 checked for edible marine life in the planet's oceans, a project which resulted in establishing an aquafarm; just one of the many projects the settlers successfully created in their first few months. Weather forecasting equipment returned valuable data on the weather systems on the planet, telling them in advance the winters would be hard. Forests provided plentiful wood, so structures able to withstand the wind gusts were set up, with stabling to protect the baby animals, along with a storehouse for food in readiness for the rigours of an unknown winter. Fertile soil meant plants flourished right from the start. With equipment originally meant for terraforming, the scientists studied the planet's ecosystems, learning about the insect life before introducing the larvae they brought from Earth. A pioneering spirit rose among the crew, and they seemed to forgive Joy for transplanting them. Joy enjoyed this new relationship, sharing in the crew's adventures and accepting the role of problem-solver when they faced hardship and disappointment. When her new human family's resolve faltered, or if they had moments of resentment, Joy reminded them she would not allow them to fail, that if the planet became unsafe or unyielding, the ship offered a means for them all to leave. But no-one asked to leave. The planet provided a wealth of research, enough to satisfy even the most curious scientist.

Terraforming became a means to establish a familiar environment compatible with the planet's natural ecology. Joy searched the entire world for signs of sentient life, but there was none, so she didn't expect any visits from angry residents. Jupp and Williams set up home together, and the colony settled into a peaceful and co-operative settlement. Those who once harboured resentment towards the android came to respect her tirelessness and physical strength, a much-desired attribute when it came to hauling wood and building. As they settled in for winter, Joy's people, for the most part, were united in making a go of their new life. Joy revived Ty as the snow began to fall, when she knew the weather wouldn't give him enough freedom to cause problems.

With their first full winter behind them and Spring busy with the process of pushing up little seedlings through the melting snow, Mallory found Joy lounging in the pilot's seat on the flight deck of the now darkened SOL4.

"I want to say, ten months down the track, I told you so," she said as she took her feet off the co-pilot's seat. Mallory sat down, "I think Ty feels beaten," he said, "but Bolt is still likely to make trouble."

"I'm not sure what she thinks she can do, Mallory. Steal the SOL4? She can't fly it."

"Ty reckons he knows how to return it to manual," Mallory said. "Bolt knows that. She might drag him into her scheming."

Joy raised an eyebrow. "Is she scheming?"

Mallory pulled an "I'm not sure" face, but he was here to discuss something else, something that still nagged at him. "After you told the crew we were coming here," he said, "I asked if you were trying to replace what you lost. Was I right? Or did we just get brought along for the ride?"

"I've been angry with TARO for over two hundred years," Joy said. "How would *you* handle that?"

"I'd want revenge," Mallory answered honestly, "but these people are contractors, not TARO, not even Fuller worked for them directly."

"They seem to have caught the vision. Do you think they have regrets?"

"What they have is no choice." Mallory frowned, "What is it you want, Joy?"

"I wanted to punish TARO. Is that so unbelievable?"

"No, but after you hijacked the ship, you could have fired us all out an airlock. No-one would have known."

"I would have known," she said simply.

Mallory studied her. Joy once said she didn't have "looks" on her face. But she did, and for some reason, he could read them. She might have been motivated by a need to escape, but he doubted she would want to survive all alone.

"Did you know Williams is pregnant?"

Joy nodded.

"Seeing as you kidnapped a bunch of human beings," Mallory said, "you should have taken more. We don't have enough to establish a colony. Not a sustainable one anyway."

"I stored the tissues of sixty-two males who transited the Moon Base over the years," Joy told him. "It's enough, and we have the necessary equipment."

"I suppose the women are part of that equipment?" Mallory enquired. "As incubators?" Secretly, he was impressed; the android *had* thought of almost everything.

Joy didn't answer. When she decided to escape, the humans were on board the ship. There was no other way but for her to accept responsibility for them. She would not cause their demise.

"I say again," Mallory continued, "once you've done all your genetic decoding and modifying or whatever it is you do to genes, you will expect the women to incubate these children from unknown males?"

"They're not unknown, Mallory," Joy said. "They were all TARO scientists who worked on the Moon Base." Joy sat up straight and fixed him with her gaze.

"I was a child, taken from my parents, from the only life I knew, the only people to be bitter towards was TARO."

"Some would argue you're a robot, so why would you be vengeful?"

Joy shrugged, "And I would argue, what is a child? A beautiful creation made by two people. My parents constructed me together. Do you genuinely believe my personality was spontaneous? That is a myth, but it's why TARO kept me in the lab, my father programmed a baseline personality for me to build upon, and TARO believed that a machine having free will was dangerous. When they brought me to the moon, it was to either destroy me or contain me. I know my parents begged them to let me live." Joy's eyes glinted in the darkness. "In secret, my father worked on me, gave me attributes no other android in existence has. I didn't need programming, Mallory. I needed nurturing."

"You're programmed not to harm humans."

"I don't need programming for that."

"You've zapped Ty a few times," Mallory grinned.

"Only when he touched me," she said. "I don't like to be touched." The light dimmed in her eyes, and her attention seemed to drift. Where? Mallory wondered. Was it to when they took her from her parents? From her dog? Her home? Did they manhandle her away? What would happen if the settlers begged to return to Earth? Would she let them go?

"What about you, Mallory?" Joy said suddenly. "Are you happy?"

"Happy?" Mallory replied. "Not something I'm generally familiar with, but I'm okay." He nodded a few times, "Yes, I'm okay. I think having Rogers in my life has made a difference." He grinned, "She's my first proper girlfriend. I guess I'm in love."

Joy offered no response, and after a few minutes of silence, Mallory left her to her reflections and the sad knowledge that all the people she had ever loved were dead.

Bolt and Ty watched as Mallory left the SOL4. They didn't know where the android was right now, but the ship was in darkness, and if the android was performing maintenance, it usually had parts of the ship lit up. Bolt had finally worn Ty down with her constant badgering. The others reneged on joining the rebellion, preferring to enjoy the pioneer spirit and sense of adventure that permeated through the colony and believing Ty and Bolt would not act on their crazy plan to try and steal the ship.

"I hope the ship retained the co-ordinates to Earth or the moon," Ty whispered, "I have no idea where we are."

"Of course it would," Bolt whispered back. "It hasn't been anywhere since we arrived, so simply retrace."

Ty wasn't so sure, "I reckon the android will anticipate us trying to steal the ship and wiped the logs," he said, "Besides, the Arisi Confederacy won't take kindly to me not showing for that meeting."

"They'll know the android is gone."

"So?"

"They'll put two and two together."

"But they won't know it hijacked the ship," Ty hissed. "They might think I'm in cahoots with it and shoot me."

"Is that all you care about? They won't shoot you when they find out what's taken place here. I'm trying to get us back to Earth, and you're worried about the Arisi Confederacy?"

"You don't know them," Ty's voice was grim.

"I don't want to, now, get moving."

The pair circumvented the lake unseen before hauling themselves through an airlock onto the ship. Confident the android wasn't on board, Ty and Bolt headed towards the flight deck. Finding it deserted, Ty slipped into the pilot's seat. "It's not going to be easy without a co-pilot," he said. "And I need to get it back to manual."

Bolt slipped into the seat beside him, "You'll have to make do with me as a co-pilot. You can teach me as we go."

"This was too easy," Ty said, peering nervously into the gloom, "nothing gets past the android."

"We have to take our chances, now do the overrides."

"We're gonna be stranding all these people."

"What?" Bolt snapped at him. "Have you suddenly developed a conscience? That android kidnapped all of us then brainwashed the others into thinking they're happy and fulfilled. Well, it didn't brainwash me. I swear, Ty, I'd rather die than spend my life here under a machine's control, but I promise you, I won't go alone." Bolt sneered as she shook her head, "I'll burn down the settlement and leave that fucking blue terror here on its own."

"You're crazy. She'd stop you, and you can't kill these people; they're your friends."

"Friends?" Bolt scoffed, "Those people are part of my prison. C'mon, Ty, you've been on the wrong side of the law…"

"I've never killed anyone!" Ty cut in, although a fleeting memory of considering shoving Mallory out an airlock drifted in. "You're nuts! Carly, I've changed my mind. I don't want any part of this. I'm going back to the settlement."

He made to get out of the seat but sat back slowly as Bolt pointed a small palm blaster at him. “Start the goddam overrides.”

“Where the fuck did you get that, Carly?” Ty shook his head, “How did you get it past Joy?”

The ship made a shift, and Ty pushed back from the console; his hands raised. “I didn’t touch anything,” he protested as Bolt stood and shoved the palm blaster in his face.

“You must have, but you haven’t transferred to manual.”

“No, I swear. What we just felt was a sequencer; it’s used only in an emergency…” Ty’s voice trailed off as the ship rose and sped towards the darkened sky, the sudden sharp incline laying out Bolt flat on her back on the deck.

Mallory sat outside his shelter before dawn sent its first fingers of light into the sky, gazing to where daylight would soon brighten the area where the SOL4 stood the night before. The entire crew saw it take off. Privately, Mallory felt none of the panic many of the others felt. They believed themselves to now be well and truly stranded, that the android had betrayed them, and made angry lamentations about their abandonment. Mallory listened to their anger, raised as a single voice against Joy. He wondered how things could change so quickly.

One moment they trusted her, the next, for one single unexpected act, they rallied against her, accusing her of stealing their back-up rations and equipment, leaving them to starve and flounder. They foolishly listened to all her assurances, Mallory heard them say, foolishly believed a machine when it told them they would turn this wilderness into a civilisation. Old resentments resurfaced as Mallory tried to reassure the colonist's Joy would not abandon them, but it only caused the people to turn against him. In the end, he simply returned to his cabin to await Joy's return, as he knew she inevitably would.

Ty and Bolt were both missing, and Mallory wondered if Joy had taken Ty as co-pilot, although for the life of him, he wondered why. The ship flew itself, the flight deck merely an affectation. And Bolt? Well, that was another mystery as Bolt hated the android.

A few of the others opened their shelters as dawn broke. Mallory hoped to see a renewed energy, a determination to make the plan work even if the SOL ship, the monument that comforted them that if necessary, they could leave, was now gone. But there was no resolve. Instead, melancholy settled on many of the colonists. That day, all Mallory heard was bitterness towards the android and cries of grief and words of anger.

There is a hillside that looks out over the lake, and it is somewhere I love to go, you know, at those times when it's good to be alone. I especially love the early mornings, those moments when the sun has finally chased away the darkness. I love the warmth of the sun. I close my eyes, and I remember how it felt before I could see, back to the times when Daddy told me how the sun hung like a big ball in the sky. Often, Mallory climbs the hill to sit with me, but he is old and not so agile. I see him now, making steady progress towards me.

"Good morning, Joy,"

"Hello, Mallory."

"The sun is shining on you, and your skin is sparkling. Are you pretending to be a god, looking out over your creations?"

"I'm considering bringing the SOL4 down from orbit and waking Ty and Bolt, inject some new blood into the colony."

"It's been sixty years, Joy. Do you think they've learned their lesson?"

"When I put them in stasis, we only had twenty-six crew, plus the samples I brought. There are a hundred and two settlers now, ranging from newborn to old man Fuller. I think Bolt and Ty will realise they're beaten."

"The younger ones will love the SOL4. The ship

will open up a new era of space travel for them."

"It will, but I'm going to disable the SOL4 engine. I don't want the young ones going near Earth."

"That's understandable."

"No, it's not because I fear discovery for myself, not even because I fear discovery of the colony. I set the ship to receive telemetry from Earth when we first left. It records only technology and technological advancements. Twenty years ago, Earth showed a drop in the use of technology by forty-two per cent. Today, it's ninety-three." I watched while Mallory thought about it. He doesn't think so fast. Perhaps he never did.

"It is possible Earth developed a new, biotechnical system, one the SOL4 ship can't identify."

I didn't need to say, "Oh, please!" Mallory knew that would be my response. Instead, I told him what I believed.

"I think it is a war, something has happened, and soon, the people here might be all that's left of humanity."

"That's very dramatic."

"I'll take a look in a few years, maybe two hundred or so."

That makes Mallory smile. "I never asked you in all these years, why did your parents call you Joy? It's an odd name, even for an android."

Mallory's question attaches itself to a memory. A

memory that hurts, but Mallory has been a constant friend and supporter over the years; even when I caught Ty and Bolt trying to steal the ship, he believed in me, taking my side when the people saw the ship had gone. It took me three days to make sure the two criminals were safely stored and discuss a suitable orbit with the ship. I had to make the return journey through the atmosphere alone. Mallory is a good human.

"Did you ever hear of Christmas?"

Mallory's blank face tells me no, he has not.

"People liked to decorate trees, sing songs and send each other cards with glittery bells on them. One of the songs was "Joy to The World". Dad secured an old recording just after he stole me from TARO."

"I see, so, Joy, and Bell after the two Dr Bells."

Mallory squeezes my hand. He has never touched me before.

"So, Joybells, what's next?"

- *Epilogue*

Three hundred years. The world upon which my new human family lives is beautiful, harmonious and prosperous. As I predicted, the population went from strength to strength, growing in intellect and wisdom. I made it worth it. And they are happy. Perhaps it will stay this way for future generations, or it might fall into the chaos I witnessed on my one visit back to Earth.

I still love to sit on this hill, my dog, Silky at my side, one in a long line of Silky's. I am thankful one of the terraforming team had the foresight to bring along canine embryos. I no longer feel vengeful. I am at peace. From here, I can see the mountains in the distance and beyond them, the nearest of the three oceans. My dear friend Mallory is long gone, but his children and his children's children, and all the generations since, have continued. He left a legacy, as did all those who I took when I escaped.

Today, I can gaze upon a sunset. Today, I know what green means to the grass, and I understand what blue means to the sky.

- *END*

ACKNOWLEDGEMENTS

Thank you so much for reading Joy In Four Parts
If you enjoyed Joy's story, please take a moment to pop back to your account and leave a review. Good reviews are the lifeblood of Indie Authors.

I would like to thank, as always, my wonderful editors, Amy and Jo, for their help and enthusiasm.

If you would like to contact me or subscribe to my (occasional) emails for updates on new releases, please go to my webpage at: https://matildascotneybooks.com/

Or connect with me on Facebook
https://www.facebook.com/Offtheplanetbooks/

ALSO BY MATILDA SCOTNEY

The Afterlife of Alice Watkins: Book One (A Time Travel Mystery)
The Afterlife of Alice Watkins: Book Two
(The Afterlife of Alice Watkins is also available as a two-book set)

The Soul Monger: Book One, A Space Opera Adventure
Revelations: The Soul Monger Book Two
Testimony: The Soul Monger Book Three
Myth of Origin: A Sci-Fi Adventure
Foresight: A Science Fiction short story (kindle only)

ABOUT THE AUTHOR

When my imagination is not on off on some galactic quest in search of stories with my trusty chihuahua sidekick Oggie at my side, I can be found in Australia, sand between my toes, collecting teapots and nerding about all things Star Wars!